The Puppies of Blossom Meadow

The Puppies of Blossom Meadow

By Catherine Coe

Book 1:
Fairy Friends

SCHOLASTIC

Published in the UK by Scholastic Children's Books, 2020
Euston House, 24 Eversholt Street, London, NW1 1DB, UK
A division of Scholastic Limited

London – New York – Toronto – Sydney – Auckland
Mexico City – New Delhi – Hong Kong

Text © Catherine Coe, 2020
Cover illustration © Andrew Farley represented by Meiklejohn, 2020
Inside illustrations © Yesenia Moises, 2020
Illustrations from *Unicorns of Blossom Wood: Believe in Magic* extract © Renée
Kurilla, 2016

The right of Catherine Coe and Yesenia Moises to be identified as the author
and illustrator of this work has been asserted by them under the Copyright,
Designs and Patents Act 1988.

ISBN 978 1407 19866 8

A CIP catalogue record for this book
is available from the British Library.

Printed by CPI Group (UK) Ltd, Croydon, CR0 4YY

Papers used by Scholastic Children's Books are made
from wood grown in sustainable forests.

1 3 5 7 9 10 8 6 4 2

www.scholastic.co.uk

For little blueberry

xxx

Chapter 1
Doggy Delight

"This is nothing like I thought it'd be!" Erin said, as she, Amber and Kayla stepped through the front door of a red-brick Victorian house.

Kayla nodded. "It's just like a home, right? Not like a dog kennels at all. I mean, apart from all the dog toys, dog collars and dog baskets!" Kayla joked. They stepped into the main room, where dogs of all shapes and sizes were sitting in dog baskets and on covered sofas.

A sausage dog scampered up to Amber, and she knelt down to stroke its sleek, brown fur. "Hello, Matt," she said, reading the dog's name tag. "Aren't you friendly? But I've never heard of a dog called Matt before!"

Kayla's dad stepped into the room behind them. "Oh, we get all sorts of dog names here," he said. "The biggest problem is remembering them all!" Kayla's dad worked at Doggy Delight, and she'd visited before, but this was the first time Kayla had been allowed to bring along her two best friends. She'd pleaded with her dad for ages to let the three of them help out at the kennels, and at last he had decided they were old enough. They were SO excited at the thought of spending the whole day surrounded by cute dogs.

"This one's my favourite," said Kayla, stroking a German Shepherd with a very pink and waggly tongue. "Poppy comes here every day while her owners are at work. Can we take her out for a walk, Dad?"

"Not yet," Kayla's dad replied. "But the three of you can come out with me later, when it's time for the mid-morning walks."

Amber hopped from foot to foot with excitement, while Erin punched the air, shouting, "Awesome!"

The three friends lived in the same tower block, twenty minutes' walk from the kennels, and they weren't allowed any pets in their flats. But Erin had loved animals ever since she was a baby and had spent summers on her grandparents' farm in

Sweden, helping to look after the sheep and hens. She knew she wanted to work with animals one day, and now she was getting the chance to try it out!

"First," Kayla's dad said, "please could the three of you clean out the storeroom? It's been ages since it was tidied."

Amber, Erin and Kayla looked at each other. Cleaning wasn't exactly what they thought they'd be doing today!

"OK, Dad," Kayla said. "As long as you promise we can take the dogs out for walks once we're done?" She gave him a wide, pleading smile.

He laughed. "Sure thing," he said. "The storeroom's in the shed at the end of the garden. Here's the key."

The three best friends made their way through the house to the back door, stroking the dogs they passed as they went.

Outside, the narrow garden was full of dog obstacles and toys. Amber skipped over a series of agility bars laid out on the grass, while Kayla and Erin walked along the stone path.

"I didn't know dogs did the hurdles too!" Amber said, panting. The hurdles was her favourite race at sports club.

She was about to try squeezing through a training tunnel when Erin called out, "Come on, Amber! The quicker we can get the storeroom cleaned, the quicker we can get back to the dogs."

Amber skipped over to her friends as they reached the storeroom. Kayla unlocked the padlock on the door and they stepped into the room. The air inside danced with specks of dust that sparkled in the sunshine coming through the window.

"ACHOO!" Kayla sneezed.

Erin looked around at the shelves crowded with dog accessories and the piles of cardboard boxes on the floor. "Your dad wasn't joking when he said it hadn't been tidied for a while!" she said to Kayla.

"I thought it'd only take a few minutes," said Kayla, sighing. She retied the two topknots that kept her black curly hair in place and offered an extra hairband to Amber. Her friend smiled gratefully and pulled back her long, brown hair into a ponytail.

Erin tucked her bobbed blonde hair behind her ears and knelt down to start on the first shelf. She began tidying the bags of dry dog food and cleaning up the spilled pellets with a dustpan and brush.

"Ooh, look, a cuddly chicken!" Amber cried, pulling down a soft toy from the top shelf. As she grabbed it, the chicken made a giggling sound. "Is it supposed to make dogs laugh?" she wondered.

Erin shook her head as she kept on cleaning. "It's for puppies to chew on, I think. It stops them from chewing on furniture."

Kayla jumped up to reach the shelf and grabbed a chicken in each hand. She shook them like maracas and started singing, "Chick, chick, chicken! Ch-ch-ch-chick, chick, chicken!" Her friends laughed as she sprang around the storeroom.

"What's this?" Amber asked, after Kayla had stopped dancing.

Erin looked up at the short green rope in Amber's hand. "That's a tug toy. My uncle's Labrador loves playing with those."

Kayla grabbed a broom and started sweeping the floor, swishing it around as if she was dancing the waltz with it.

Erin finished sorting the dog-food shelf and moved on to the next one above it. Behind her, Amber opened a cupboard filled with dog-grooming supplies. As she moved some brushes to the top of the cupboard so she could clean the shelf, she felt something up there, and tiptoed to grab it.

"Look!" Amber said, spinning around to her friends.

"What is it now, Amber?" Erin said. "We'll never get this done if you keep stopping to look at stuff!"

Kayla swept over to Amber to take a look. "It's just an old collar."

"Maybe . . ." Amber said. "But it looks different." She blew the dust off the collar and the purple fabric sparkled.

Erin came over to see it too. "Blossom," she said, reading the name tag. "That's a lovely name for a dog."

Kayla frowned. "Dad's never mentioned
a dog named Blossom being here. And he
tells me about *all* the dogs that come to
stay."

The shiny silver name tag spun around
on its chain, and Erin and Kayla reached
out at the same time to hold it still again.

"Did you feel that?" Amber asked,
looking down at their hands on the collar.
It was suddenly tingling and warm, as if

it were alive. The next moment, white sparkles started bouncing out from the collar and whirling around in the air, like they were surrounded by a beautiful spinning firework.

Erin let out a shriek as her feet lifted, and she saw Amber and Kayla were rising up too. The three friends stared at each other as they were whisked upwards, their eyes wide and amazed. Soon they were surrounded by so many sparkles that they couldn't see the storeroom any more!

"What's happening?" Kayla yelped as she gripped the trembling collar.

"I don't know!" Erin gasped. "But hold on tight!"

Chapter 2

Welcome to Blossom Meadow

Amber couldn't help but hold her breath as she was spun around and around. And then, as quickly as it had started, the sparkles surrounding them disappeared, and Amber realized her feet were on the ground again. "What just happened?" she whispered, finally breathing once more.

"More importantly, where are we?" Erin yelled.

The friends blinked over and over as they looked around. They definitely weren't in the storeroom any more. They were outside, in a field covered with tiny white daisies that stretched as far as their eyes could see. It was warm and sunny, with a gentle breeze that smelt of fresh air and flowers.

"H-h-how did we get out here?" Kayla stuttered. She didn't recognize where they were at all. And then she spun around and saw what was behind her. Amber and Erin were nowhere to be seen . . . but there were two puppies staring at her – a black terrier with a white stomach and a golden Labrador.

"Hey, where are you?" Kayla called out to her two best friends.

"I'm right here," the Labrador said, and Kayla's legs wobbled in shock. That was Erin's voice!

Kayla looked down at herself, and nearly collapsed completely. She didn't see her human legs in black jeans, but brown furry doggy legs! She was standing on all fours, she realized, and she was panting – just like a dog!

The black terrier spun in a circle. "Um ... I think ... we're dogs?" *The terrier is Amber!* Kayla realized as she recognized her voice too.

"You look like a cockapoo, Kayla," Erin said. She suddenly felt her tail wagging back and forth, and it wouldn't seem to stop!

Kayla twisted around, and sure enough, her body was very fluffy and brown, with a curled-up tail. She yelped, but it came out more like a bark!

Erin's head shook back and forth, her golden ears flapping. "This isn't real. It can't be!"

"Maybe it's a dream," Amber said, lifting her black paws to feel her furry face. "And if so, then it might be the best dream I've ever had!"

Erin nudged her nose into the grass between them. The Blossom collar lay there, the name tag glittering in the sunshine. "The collar. It must be magical!" she said. "I don't think this is a dream at all." She remembered how they'd been whisked up into the air from the storeroom.

"But we're *dogs*!" said Kayla, as she peered at her friends more closely. "Actually, I think we're puppies! I've never heard of magic like this. Rabbits are supposed to come out of hats. Girls aren't supposed to turn into dogs!"

Her friends laughed at Kayla's joke and Amber quickly got the giggles. She bounced up and down, just like she did a lot as a girl, except now she had black ears that were waggling.

"Hey there, what's so funny?" came a twittering voice above them. The puppies looked up and blinked in surprise. A purple-tipped butterfly was talking to them!

Erin's mouth gaped open. "Um . . .
m-magic!" she said. "I mean . . . w-we like
magic. Don't we?" She glanced around
at Amber and Kayla, hoping they'd help
her out. But her friends were staring at
her. They'd never seen Erin lost for words
before!

"Oh, I LOVE magic," said the butterfly.
"Can you do any magic tricks?" She
fluttered down to land on Kayla's shoulder
and peered into her big brown eyes. "What
are you, anyway?" she asked, before any of
the friends could reply.

"Wh-what do you mean?" Erin stuttered
again.

The butterfly flapped her wings quickly.
"I mean, I've never seen animals like you
before!"

"Oh, we're dogs," Amber explained.
"Puppies!" She let out a little bark as if that

might help them seem less strange to the insect.

The butterfly fluttered over to Amber's shiny black nose. "Oooooh, I've heard of dogs, but I've never seen one! Never mind – that doesn't matter. I'm a butterfly, by the way. My name's Chloe. Welcome to Blossom Meadow!"

Blossom Meadow? thought Kayla. *Like the collar!*

The three best friends smiled and told Chloe their names.

"If you're new here," Chloe said, "let me show you around!" She shot up into the air, her wings moving so fast they were a blur.

Erin ducked down to slip the Blossom collar over her head for safekeeping, then scampered to catch up with Amber and Kayla. They were trying to run while also looking upwards, following Chloe in the sky. As they hadn't been puppies for very long, they weren't finding it easy. Running on four legs was very different from two!

"That's Honeysuckle Hill," Chloe called out as she pointed a wing to the right of the daisy field. A hill rose up, covered in pretty yellow flowers. When Kayla breathed in, she could smell the sweet scent of the honeysuckle, as strong as perfume. "And that's Poppy Place." Chloe nodded towards a poppy field to their left, filled with bright poppies the colour of carrots. "Can you see that giant hedge in the distance? That's the Great Hedge and the border of Blossom Meadow. Beyond that is Blossom Wood."

Amber squinted, but all she could see was the faintest brown line on the horizon. Blossom Meadow was gigantic!

Chloe swerved left in the sky towards the poppies. "Let's go and see if my friend George is in. He'd love to meet you!"

The puppies scampered through Poppy Place, dodging left and right so they didn't trample any of the beautiful flowers that towered around them. Erin was looking out for George, guessing he'd be a butterfly who lived amongst the poppies, but soon they reached the edge of the poppy field. Beyond it was a big area of brown soil.

"George lives *here*?" Erin said without thinking first. It was the least pretty place they'd seen in Blossom Meadow so far.

"Of course!" chirped Chloe. "All the badgers do!"

Amber gasped. She'd never seen a badger before, except on TV, and that didn't really count.

Chloe fluttered down to one of the holes in the dry, dusty soil. "Cooee, George," she said. "I've got some new friends here that I think you'd love to meet!"

There was a scuffling sound and the next moment, a black-and-white pointed badger's nose popped out of the hole. His eyes widened. "Dogs!" he yelped. "What a surprise to have your sort in the wood. But welcome . . . you're very welcome!" George leapt out of the burrow and lumbered over to shake the paws of each of the puppies.

Kayla grinned as George reached over to take her paw. He seemed like a very polite badger!

"I've been showing them around," Chloe
explained to George. She spun up to look
at the sun and squeaked. "But I must go
now. I'm late for my salsa dance class!
George, can you be a dear and look after
the puppies?"

Kayla spotted a frown appearing on
George's face. "Don't worry," she said
quickly. "We can show ourselves around.

I'm sure you've very busy, Mr Badger."

"Oh, do call me George! But you're right – I'm in the middle of making a new bed of leaves in my den. Are you sure you'll be all right without me?"

Erin nodded. "We'll be fine!" She secretly wanted to be alone with Kayla and Amber again, and she was sure they felt the same.

"In that case, have fun," Chloe called, as she zoomed up into the blue cloudless sky. "I'm sure I'll bump into you later!"

The puppies waved goodbye to Chloe and George, and then scampered away

across the badger burrows. They could see a stream in the distance, lined with blossoming fruit trees. The friends crossed a meadow filled with violets and leapt around in the flowers, barking happily.

"This is AMAZING," said Amber, wagging her white-tipped tail. "We can go anywhere!"

"And it's beautiful too," Erin added with a skip. The three friends were used to being surrounded by concrete buildings and busy traffic. This was the exact opposite!

They reached the stream and found a wooden bridge leading across it. At either

end, the bridge was surrounded by a carpet of bright yellow buttercups, all soft and springy under their paws. The friends followed a path beside the stream on the other side that was edged with tall, turret-like flowers in pink, purple and red.

"Can you hear that?" asked Kayla, skidding to a stop.

Amber and Erin turned to her. "What?" they said together, pricking up their ears to listen.

Kayla scrunched up her eyes to concentrate. "It sounds like someone crying," she said, hearing the light sobbing noise again.

"I can hear it too!" Erin barked. "Whoever it is sounds really upset. Come on – we have to find them!"

Chapter 3

A Tiny Surprise

Amber, Erin and Kayla started looking around the flowers nearby, their wet puppy noses to the ground, their ears standing tall to listen. Every so often, they would hear a sob, but they couldn't find anything along the path beside the stream.

"Are we imagining it?" Amber wondered, as they reached the end of the path.

"Not if we can *all* hear it!" said Erin, shaking her golden head.

As if to agree, another squeaking sob came, a bit louder this time. Kayla cocked her head to one side. "Maybe it's further away than we think," she said. "Aren't dogs supposed to have great hearing?"

Erin nodded. Kayla was right! "So we need to follow the sound," Erin said. "It must be this way, if it's getting louder."

Amber dashed out in front as they entered a vast patch of sunflowers. The stalks towered over them, at least four times as high as the puppies. "Please stay close so we don't lose each other!" Erin called out, and Amber circled back around. The sobbing grew louder and louder, and the puppies knew they were headed in the right direction. Then they emerged from the shade of the sunflowers out into

green grass peppered with bright, beautiful
bluebells.

"It's coming from over there," Kayla
whispered, pointing to the left edge of the
stunning purple-blue flowers.

The puppies tried to tiptoe towards the
crying, in case they scared whoever it was.

"Hello?" Amber called out gently.

"Who's that?" came a male voice that
sounded like a tinkling bell.

Amber looked at Kayla and Erin for help.

"We're puppies!" Erin replied without thinking.

The friends heard a loud gasp from a clutch of bluebell stalks.

"What Erin means to say is: we've come to see if you're OK," said Kayla. "We won't hurt you."

"Yes," Erin agreed. "Please come out. If you're in trouble, we can help you!"

"You can't!" the voice rang out before bursting into sobs again.

Amber's eyes filled with tears at the sound of the crying. "We'll try our best," she said. "We promise! And my mum always says that a problem shared is a problem halved."

"I wonder what it is?" Erin whispered to Kayla. "Another butterfly? A bird maybe? Or an insect?"

The bluebell stalks shook a little. Something was moving behind them.

"We promise we won't come too close," Kayla said gently. She shuffled backwards to give the creature room and gestured to her friends to do the same.

The stalks rustled some more . . . and a small face peeked out.

The puppies had to put their paws over their mouths to stop themselves from gasping. It wasn't an animal or insect at all. It was a fairy!

He tiptoed out and looked up at the puppies with his wide, navy eyes. They took in his stunning golden wings, pointy ears and blue-tinged skin.

"I've never met a dog before," he gasped, still staring.

"That's what Chloe said," Kayla replied.

The fairy took another step forward.

"You know Chloe?"

All three puppies nodded.

"She's been showing us around Blossom Meadow," Amber told him. "It's amazing! You're so lucky to live here!"

Kayla nudged Amber. Maybe the fairy didn't feel so lucky if he'd been crying.

"Will you tell us what's wrong?" Kayla asked in her kindest voice.

The fairy slumped down to the ground, sitting cross-legged on the grass.

"It's the bluebells," he said. "Creatures keep picking them! We can use magic to stop them being taken most of the time, but our magic fades as the day goes on and we have to go to bed at dusk to recharge it. When we wake up in the morning, there are always a few more bluebell patches missing." The fairy sniffed and hung his head.

"Can't you just ask the others to stop taking them?" Erin said, frowning.

He looked up and put his chin in his hands. "Oh no, we can't do that. We don't know who it is, and anyway, it wouldn't be very nice. It's the fairy code: be kind, be caring, be nice!"

"Hmmm," said Amber thoughtfully. "How about we ask them to stop on your behalf?"

The fairy shook his head. "That wouldn't be very nice either! No, I don't see what we can do. We understand that everyone wants to decorate their home with bluebells – they're so pretty. The problem is, if it carries on like this, we'll have to leave Blossom Meadow!"

"Then we'll try to help another way," Kayla said. "Without telling everyone to stop."

"Yes, we'll sort this out for you," Erin added, standing up straighter with her golden chest pushed forward. "Leave it with us!"

"Oh, really? You are kind! It's my birthday tomorrow – AND my twin sister's – and it'd be the best birthday present to wake up and see no more bluebells missing."

Tomorrow? thought Amber, gulping. How

were they going to work out what to do so quickly? But Erin had promised now! "Umm, couldn't you move somewhere else in Blossom Meadow?" Amber asked, trying to think of another way to solve the problem.

"Oh no!" the fairy squeaked. "We're bluebell fairies. We need the bluebells for our magic. And this is Bluebell Grove. These are the only bluebells in Blossom Meadow, so we can't live anywhere else!" As if to prove his point, a few fairy heads suddenly popped out shyly from behind bluebell stalks, their faces sad.

"I'm sorry," said Amber, feeling bad for not realizing that.

"We'll fix it," Erin repeated. "Right away!" The puppies waved goodbye to the fairies and turned to go, but heard another soft voice behind them.

"Bran, who were you talking to?" it said.

They spun around again and saw that one of the other fairies had stepped out fully to join the first fairy, this one with flowing blue hair to the waist.

"This is my twin sister, Sen," Bran said. He took Sen's hands and turned to her. "The puppies are going to stop the bluebells being picked for us," Bran told Sen. "Won't that be wonderful?"

Sen beamed and her blue face shone like a gem. "Really?" she said. "Oh, thank you!"

Kayla gulped. They couldn't let the fairies down now. But how would they fix this?

Chapter 4

A Plan

The three best friends waved to the fairies and scampered away. When they got to the bridge of buttercups, Kayla stopped and barked at Amber and Erin to do the same.

"Where are we going?" Kayla said. "We don't have a plan yet!"

Amber shrugged and made to start

running again. "I don't know, but there's hardly any time!"

"Kayla's right," said Erin. "There's no point in us just running around without any idea what we're doing."

Kayla sat down in the shade of a pear tree by the stream and began munching on a fallen ripe pear.

"There isn't time to eat, either!" Erin told her.

"I'm thinking," Kayla explained. "And I can't do that on an empty stomach."

Amber grinned at her friend. The puppy version of Kayla was very similar to the girl version! But Amber was too worried to eat. She couldn't even sit down. "What are we going to do to help the fairies?" she said, spinning around as if she might get the answer that way.

Erin lay down beside Kayla in the soft

grass and put her head in her paws. "Well, we need to stop everyone stealing the bluebells. If we can't tell people not to do it, how about we stop them from being able to?"

Kayla's fluffy brown head creased into a frown. "But how?"

"A fence," said Erin. "We can build one to guard the bluebells!"

"Ooh, good idea," Amber said.

"What's a good idea?" said a light voice above them.

The puppies jerked their necks to look upwards and spotted Chloe zooming down.

"Um, that we keep on exploring!" Erin said quickly. "Blossom Meadow is amazing!"

Chloe beamed and settled down on a twig between the puppies. "Oh, I'm SO happy you're having fun. Shall I come with you?"

Kayla gulped, but luckily Chloe added,

"Oh no, I can't! I promised I'd help the bees deliver their honey. Will you be all right continuing without me?"

"Yes!" Erin said (a little too enthusiastically, Kayla thought).

"We mean, we wish you could join us, but we're fine by ourselves," Kayla added.

Amber clapped her black paws together. "I'd love to meet the bees," she said, imagining them buzzing all about, plucking up pollen and making honey.

Kayla glared at Amber. Had she forgotten about the fairies already? If they went to meet the bees, they'd have even less time. "Maybe we could do that tomorrow?" Kayla suggested.

"Of course!" said Chloe. She gave a couple of flaps of her purple-tipped wings and shot up into the air. "See you soon, by the sun, stars or moon!"

"So we need to make a fence," Erin said, as soon as she was absolutely sure Chloe was out of hearing distance. She jumped up and started collecting all the twigs lying about on the grass near them. "Come on!"

Soon, the puppies were holding as many twigs as they could fit into their mouths. They sped off back towards Bluebell Grove, Amber at the front. Panting, they dropped the twigs on the ground and looked around at the bright blue flowers. "We're going to need a LOT more twigs," Kayla said.

Erin nodded. "I know, but we can do this. There are loads more twigs around!"

Amber had already begun planting the twigs into the ground like tent pegs, keeping them close to each other to stop creatures slipping between them. "We could weave long grasses around the twigs when we're done," she suggested.

"That's a great idea," Kayla said.

"See – we'll have this fixed in no time!"
Erin said, smiling. The three best friends
knew they were really quite different to
each other, but they always worked well as
a team. Even their teachers said so.

"Eeeeeeeeeehhhhhh!" came a tiny high-
pitched scream from behind the half-built
fence. The next moment, Bran shot over

it, flapping his beautiful golden wings. "What's happening?" he shrieked.

"We're building a fence," said Amber. "This will stop everyone picking the bluebells!" She smiled at the fairy, but he did not smile back. In fact, his dark blue eyes were wide with horror.

"We'll be like prisoners!" Bran said.

Erin tilted her golden head to one side. "But you can just fly over it. Like you did just now!"

"No, no, no," Bran mumbled to himself. "I mean, I very much appreciate all the work you've done, but we can't be kept separate like this. It won't be at all good for our fairy karma. Plus we're happy for everyone else to *see* the bluebells, just not take them!"

The puppies all hung their heads. "We're sorry," said Kayla. "We didn't think of that. We were just trying to help . . ."

"Oh, I know," Bran said. "I shouldn't have screamed. I'm so sorry. But please can you find another way?"

"We'll try," Amber said as she started plucking the twigs out of the ground. She didn't want to upset the fairy any more than they already had!

Bran flew to the end of the half-made fence. "I can take the twigs out," he said. "I feel bad for all the work you've done. You weren't to know."

"OK," Erin said. "We'll get going and work on a new plan. Don't worry – we'll figure this out somehow!"

The puppies were running across the field of violets when they spotted a familiar black-and-white figure bounding towards them.

"Oh, goodie gumbles, I was hoping to

find you!" George said. "Where are you going in such a rush?"

"Nowhere!" Erin replied quickly, which was kind of true. They still didn't have a new plan to save the bluebells and had been dashing about aimlessly for ages.

George beamed. "Oh, marvellous! You'll have time to come to mine for a spot of afternoon tea then, won't you?"

"Umm . . ." Kayla started, but she couldn't think of an excuse.

"And I won't take no for an answer!" George told them. "Come on!"

Moments later, the three puppies were sitting on tree-trunk chairs inside George's burrow. George was bringing out all kinds of cakes, from cherry muffins to apricot tarts, but the puppies were hardly looking at the treats.

They were too distracted by the flowers

that filled every corner of George's home –
bluebells! He had them in the fireplace, in a
vase on the table, even hanging from
the ceiling.

"Beautiful, aren't they?" George said,
noticing them looking. "I always go past
Bluebell Grove on my evening walk to pick
a few."

Amber nudged Kayla beside her. "We
should say something," Amber mouthed
while George's back was turned.

"No!" hissed Kayla, her mouth half-
full with an iced bun. "We can't break the
fairies' code!"

"But taking the fairies' bluebells is
like stealing the cushions or toys from
someone else's house," Erin whispered
when George disappeared into the
kitchen.

Amber's silky black ears drooped. "We've

got to do something." She had a toffee
apple in her paw, but she'd only nibbled at
it. She just didn't feel hungry.

Erin leapt up from the table as George
returned. "Thanks so much for the
afternoon tea," she said. "But we've got
to go and ... um ... help the fairies with
something. It's a secret, for the twins'
birthday tomorrow."

George looked at the table. "But you've
hardly eaten a thing! Don't you like my
cakes?" His face sagged as he stared at the
plates piled with goodies.

"It's all delicious," said Kayla. "I wish I could eat more, really! But we have to go."

An idea pinged into Amber's head like a starburst. "I know – why don't you save everything for the fairy twins' birthday? I'm sure they'd love all these cakes."

"What a wonderful idea!" George beamed again. "I'd love to make the fairies happy. They've been looking quite sad lately, and I just can't work out why . . ."

Chapter 5

Flower Power

Outside George's burrow, the sun was dipping behind the tops of the trees in the distance.

"We don't have long!" said Amber, her ears flapping with panic. "Not if we want to get home before night-time. But . . ." For the first time since they'd arrived in Blossom Meadow, Amber thought about what might be happening at home. They'd been gone for hours. "Your dad must be so worried already!" Amber said to Kayla. "Do you think he's told our parents we're missing? Oh no!"

Kayla wondered what her dad would be thinking. Surely he'd been going out of his mind with worry. Unless he thought they were just taking a VERY long time to clean the storeroom. Which wouldn't actually be that surprising, considering how dirty it had been.

"Do you think it's the same time at home?" Erin wondered. They were supposed to be having a dog-themed sleepover at Kayla's that night and she didn't want to miss out on that! They'd already picked out all the doggy films they wanted to watch, and they were going to bake dog-shaped biscuits together, using a cookie-cutter Amber had got for her birthday last week.

Kayla shrugged. "Dunno! But we can't leave yet, can we?"

"We don't even know if we *can* leave," Erin said.

"That's true!" Kayla added. "We might be stuck here – although it's probably the best place to be stuck!" she joked. "I'm not sure I ever want to leave anyway!"

Amber's tail trembled with worry. She loved Blossom Meadow already, but she wasn't sure she liked the idea of never going home!

Erin saw Amber's eyes filling with tears and reached over to stroke her head. "Please don't worry. I'm sure we can use the collar to get back, just like when we came here. But you're right, Kayla, there's no way we can leave yet!"

The puppies left the badger's burrow behind and dashed across Poppy Place, making sure to avoid trampling any of the flowers. In patches, the poppies grew so thick it was like running through a forest! Amber was trying to forget about home for now, but the masses of flowers reminded her so much of her grandma's garden, which ran wild with flowers that seemed to grow overnight. Her grandma's house was always filled with the flowers, yet the garden never looked bare.

Amber skidded to a stop as a thought popped into her head.

"What's wrong?" Kayla asked.

Amber didn't answer straight away, but stared up at the long poppy stems.

"Amber?" Erin said, tugging at her friend with a paw.

"Poppies!" Amber said at last.

"Yes, we know these are poppies," Erin said, trying her best not to get annoyed. They were used to Amber being a bit dreamy, but they didn't have time for this.

"No, I mean that poppies might be the answer. And other wildflowers too. Just not bluebells!"

Kayla twitched her little brown nose. "What do you mean?"

Amber spun on the spot as her idea came together in her head. "Bluebells take a year to grow back when you cut them. And they take even longer to grow from seeds! But poppies don't, I'm sure of it. And daisies too."

Kayla did a little hop. "You mean there are other flowers here that can be picked! Ones that will grow back quickly?"

"Exactly!" Amber said. She started examining the patch of orange poppies in front of her and plucked just a few so that she didn't leave the area too bare.

"Are we taking these to the fairies?" Erin asked, joining in with the picking. "To cheer them up?"

"No," Amber said, "although that's a nice idea. No, we're going to show the creatures in Blossom Meadow that other wildflowers can look just as nice as bluebells!"

The three best friends worked quickly but carefully, first picking flowers from Poppy Place, and then moving on to Daisy Heath and Honeysuckle Hill. Sweet smells filled their nostrils as they gathered the

flowers gently between their teeth. The sun
dipped closer to the horizon and a perfect
half-moon was rising upwards in the
darkening blue sky.

Kayla paused for a moment to stare
all around her. Blossom Meadow was so
beautiful, it almost took her breath away.
She told herself she'd have to paint a

picture of this exact scene when they got home. IF they got home. She hoped so — no matter how gorgeous Blossom Meadow was, she couldn't imagine being separated from her dad.

"We have so many flowers! Now what?" said Erin through the stems in her mouth. "I don't think I can hold any more!"

Amber gazed at the picked flowers and nodded. "Now we head to Bluebell Grove!" Amber replied, a twinkle in her shiny black eyes. She turned and started to run. Erin chased after Amber as she scampered away, with Kayla at the back of the pack.

Bright white fireflies spun around them in the purple darkness of dusk, almost as if the pretty insects were guiding the way on purpose. They raced towards the stream and found the bridge edged with

buttercups – although the yellow flowers were hardly visible now it was almost night-time.

It was almost dark when they got to Bluebell Grove, aside from the fireflies that flitted around like shooting stars in the air. There was no sign of the fairies. Kayla guessed they'd already gone to bed to recharge their magic, like Bran had told them.

Amber began to worry. Maybe no one would come along here tonight on their evening walk, and then her plan wouldn't work! She arranged the flowers they'd picked into beautiful bunches, which helped distract her mind from the worrisome thoughts bouncing around. Kayla and Erin joined in, and for once the three best friends didn't chat and laugh together. They were all too nervous for that.

Kayla tied the bunches of flowers with long strands of grass, even making little bows on each one.

"How long should we wait here?" Erin asked, hopping from paw to paw. "Maybe we should go and *find* the creatures rather than standing around here for them . . ."

"But then we'd have to run around with all these flowers, and they'd get ruined," Kayla said.

Amber nodded. "Let's wait just a bit longer." She could feel her heart beating madly, and squinted into the distance, hoping for a glimpse of an animal . . .

And there one was! No, two, in fact. A sleek brown deer and her fawn, strolling slowly along the lane that led to Bluebell Grove. The animals slowed down as they drew closer to the puppies.

"Who are you?" the mother deer asked them.

"We're puppies!" Erin explained. "We're visiting Blossom Meadow."

The fawn shuffled backwards, her eyes wide.

"Please don't be frightened," Amber said softly. "We've made these bunches of wildflowers to give to anyone who passes."

The mother deer frowned. "But why?" she asked.

Amber stared at the flowers in her paw. "Because . . . they look pretty."

"And all these flowers grow back really quickly!" Kayla jumped in to help her friend. "I don't know whether you were going to pick the bluebells tonight, but did you know they take a year to regrow?"

The mother deer put a hoof to her mouth and gasped. "I had no idea!"

The puppies all nodded solemnly.

"The bluebells always look so lovely around our home," the deer went on. "But it doesn't seem right to pick them if they've taken so long to grow."

"That's what we thought too!" said Erin.

Amber reached out to pass the flowers in her paw to the deer. "So will you take these instead?"

The deer beamed. "Of course. Thank you! These look just as beautiful. But where did you get them?"

Amber opened her mouth to explain, and then realized she couldn't remember exactly where they'd got all the flowers. She looked at Kayla and Erin with panic in her eyes.

"We got the poppies from Poppy Place, the daisies from Daisy Heath and those tiny yellow flowers from Honeysuckle Hill,"

Erin said quickly, easily remembering their journey in her mind. "You just have to be careful not to take too many from one patch," she added.

"There are the buttercups around the bridge as well," Kayla remembered. "But we didn't pick any of those today."

"Buttercup Bridge, you mean?" the deer asked. "Oh, I'm not sure the trolls living there would like that!"

Trolls? thought Kayla, looking at the surprised faces of Erin and Amber. She guessed what her friends were thinking: *There are trolls living here as well as fairies?*

The fawn nestled her head into her mother's side. "Don't worry, darling," the deer said. "The trolls are friendly, remember?" She turned to Kayla, Erin and Amber. "Thank you for the flowers. I'll make sure not to pick any more bluebells again!"

With that, she and the fawn trotted off, and the puppies looked at each other, grinning.

"It worked!" Amber cried. "It really worked!"

Chapter 6

Fairy Cakes

The three friends bounced up and down,
smiling and cheering, but they didn't
have time to celebrate for long. Three
foxes came along, then a family of mice
and a couple of magpies. The puppies
talked to each new group of animals and
offered them the wildflower bunches, then
explained how long it took for the bluebells

to grow. All the creatures were surprised,
and vowed to only pick the flowers in
Blossom Meadow that grew quickly from
now on.

More and more creatures passed – birds
and beavers and butterflies and badgers,
voles and rabbits and crickets and frogs.
Soon the puppies had just one bunch of
wildflowers left.

"I don't think any more animals
are coming," Kayla said. "It's properly

night-time now!"

Erin held up the last flowers in the light of the fireflies. "But what should we do with these?"

Amber smiled. "We could leave them as a birthday present for the fairies?" she suggested.

"That's a lovely idea!" Kayla told her friend.

They tiptoed towards the bluebells so they could leave the wildflowers where the fairies would find them.

Erin laid the flowers down just by the bluebell stalk where they'd first met Bran.

"Happy birthday!" she said. She'd meant to say it as a whisper, but it came out more like a shout. *Ooops!* she thought.

"Is it morning already?" murmured a sleepy fairy voice. Bran stepped out from between the bluebell stalks, rubbing his eyes.

"We're so sorry!" Amber said. "It's still night-time, and we didn't mean to wake you."

"Oh, I couldn't sleep anyway!" said Bran. "I never can, the night before my birthday!"

Erin smiled at the little fairy. She was always like that before her birthday too.

Kayla pointed at the flowers. "We were

just leaving these for you and Sen as a birthday present."

Bran knelt down to scoop the flowers up in his tiny arms. "Oh, they're beautiful, thank you!"

"And we've fixed the bluebell problem!" Erin told him.

"We hope so, anyway," Amber added. "We've shown the creatures the other sorts of flowers you can pick here – the ones that grow back quickly. And we told them how long bluebells take to grow. I really hope you won't have to worry about your bluebells being taken now."

Bran leapt into the air. "That's wonderful news! Thank you, puppies, from the bottom of my fairy heart. What great friends you are." He fluttered his wings as he landed again. "Oh, you must come to our birthday party tomorrow!"

"Yes please!" Erin said, but Amber and Kayla looked at her. They didn't think they should stay here overnight. What would their parents think then?!

"We'll try our best," Kayla said. Maybe they *would* be able to return tomorrow, but she didn't want to make a promise they couldn't keep.

Bran spun on the spot. "Wait there a minute!"

The puppies looked at each other as the fairy disappeared between the bluebell stalks once more. Seconds later, Bran appeared again, balancing three bright purple fairy cakes in his hands.

"Just in case you can't come, take these!" he said. "It's my way of saying thank you, for everything you did today." He handed the little cakes to the puppies, who swallowed them in one gulp.

They tasted better than any cake Kayla had ever eaten, and she was sure it made her skin tingle as she swallowed. *Maybe they're magical*, she thought.

As if he'd read her mind, Bran said, "They're sprinkled with fairy magic, so now you must make a wish!"

Amber knew right away what she was going to wish for. *I wish to get home safely*, she thought.

Bran yawned loudly, stretching his arms up high.

"We'll leave now and let you try to get some sleep," Kayla said. Bran couldn't be exhausted for his birthday!

"I think that's a good idea," Bran said. "Thank you again for all your help. See you soon, by the sun, stars or moon!" He waved goodbye and disappeared behind the flowers again.

"Goodbye," whispered the puppies. They scampered away quietly to the path by the stream until they were hidden by the tall, bright flowers that lined it. Erin took off the collar from her neck and laid it on the ground between them.

"Let's all hold it at the same time, like before," Erin said.

They did as Erin suggested and reached their paws out for the collar. It seemed to tingle under their grip! The next moment, they were being lifted up, just like before, but this time they were surrounded by purple sparkles, not white ones. Erin tried not to scream as they were spun about. She

could no longer see Blossom Meadow – just sparkling colours all around her.

Amber held her breath as they were whisked up, up, up . . . and then she felt herself floating down again. She only let her breath out when she could feel land under her paws. Except – they weren't paws any more, but feet. She was a girl again, and as the sparkles from the collar died away, Amber saw they were back in the storeroom.

"Hey, it isn't night-time here," said Kayla, looking out of the window. Then she looked back at the storeroom. It was so clean, it gleamed! "How did that happen?" she wondered, staring around her.

"Oh, that was my wish!" Erin said. "After all our work in Blossom Meadow, I didn't think we would want to finish cleaning this room!" Erin put the collar back on top of the cupboard where Amber had found it, then shook her arms and legs out as she got used to being a girl again.

Amber smiled. "My wish came true too! I wished that we would get back here safely!"

"What did you wish for, Kayla?" Erin asked.

Kayla bit her lip. "I can't say, because it

hasn't come true yet. But I'll tell you if it does!" She desperately wanted to tell her friends that she'd wished they'd be able to return to Blossom Wood tomorrow, but she knew sharing a wish before it was granted meant it wouldn't come true. That was what her grandpa always told her, anyway!

A knock on the storeroom door made the three girls jump. Kayla's dad opened the door and beamed. "Wow, you've done an incredible job in here. And so quickly too! Shall we take some of the dogs out for a walk now?"

"Yes please!" the girls replied together.

Maybe no time passed at all while we were gone, Kayla thought. *That* must *be what happened, if Dad thinks we worked so fast!*

"And if you'd like to, you can all come back tomorrow," Kayla's dad added. "You've worked so hard today, and I promise there'll be less cleaning!"

The three best friends nodded and grabbed each other's hands. "We'd love to!" Erin said. She knew her friends were thinking the same thing as her. Maybe if they came back tomorrow, they'd get to visit Blossom Meadow again!

Word Search

Can you find the six hidden animals
within this wordsearch?

X	R	A	B	B	I	T	K	G	B
E	F	H	N	J	M	V	W	T	U
B	A	D	G	E	R	S	A	U	T
E	D	O	I	K	C	K	F	B	T
A	P	R	X	N	J	D	R	L	E
V	H	V	B	R	G	Q	O	Y	R
E	G	C	U	F	E	P	G	Z	F
R	F	X	T	D	K	E	J	M	L
U	Q	W	H	I	S	O	Y	A	Y
C	R	I	C	K	E	T	S	N	Z

★ Badger   ★ Beaver   ★ Butterfly

★ Cricket   ★ Frog   ★ Rabbit

Spot the Difference

Can you spot five things that are
different in these pictures?

Spot the Difference Answers

Puppy Pairs

Can you match each girl with their puppy forms?

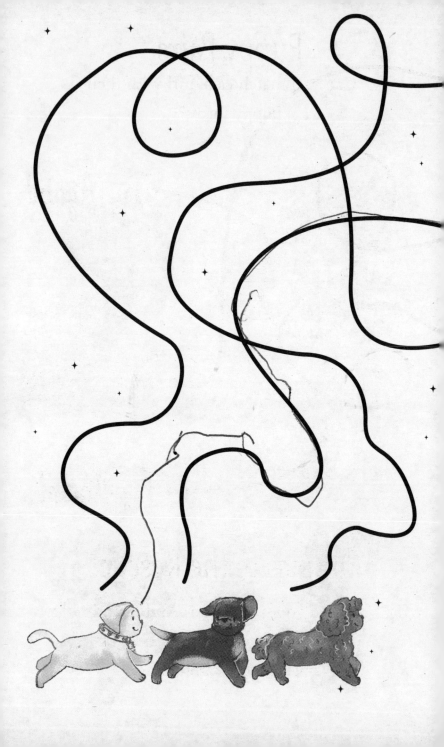

Try Again!

Try Again!

Puppies to the Rescue!

Can you help Kayla, Amber and
Erin find the missing bluebells by
picking the right path?

Follow the Sound!

Can you help Amber, Erin and Kayla
find out who's calling to them?

Time to Decorate!

Can you help Kayla, Amber and Erin
make these collars sparkle again?

You could add stars, jewels and flowers!

Did You Know?

 Although Kayla, Amber and Erin are constantly on the go throughout the story, puppies need to take a lot of naps and usually get around 15-20 hours of sleep per day – sleep is important for a young pup's developing brain.

 Like humans, puppies tend to lose their first set of teeth.

 Some puppies are born green!

Some puppies are born as identical twins.

Kayla Fact File

Want to get to know Kayla better? Here are some fun facts about her . . .

Name: Kayla Akuffo

Age: 9

Family: Lives with her dad (no brothers or sisters)

Favourite dog: German Shepherd

Transforms into: Cockapoo

Favourite hobby: Drawing

Favourite book: *Dog Man* by Dav Pilkey

Likes: Eating and making her friends laugh

Dislikes: Going to bed!

Meet

The Owls of Blossom Wood

in these magical books

Meet

The Unicorns of Blossom Wood

in these magical books

Turn over for a sneak peek of a
Blossom Wood adventure!

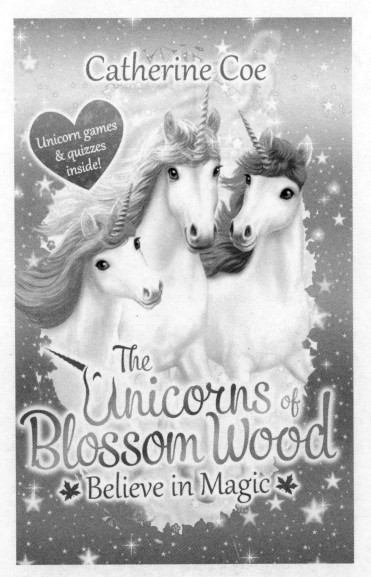

Chapter 2

Blossom Wood

After a few seconds, the bright light began to fade. Lei was the first to open her eyes, and the sight was so shocking, she found she couldn't speak for a moment. She stood on a mountain, with a beautiful woodland landscape stretching out below her – filled with blossoming trees in every direction. She could see a glimmering lake in the distance, edged by willow trees, and a

winding river rushing towards it. Closer by was a tree much taller than the rest, with a curved trunk which Lei thought looked like a crescent moon. The air buzzed with the sound of animals and birds chirping and whistling as they went about their daily business.

"Where ARE we?" Lei asked, looking all around. That was when she noticed something was different. VERY different. Where her feet used to be, there were shiny hooves. And her legs had changed too – they looked like the furry white legs of a horse!

She stumbled backwards – on her hind legs – and saw the backs of two white horses beside her. "C–Cora, Isabelle, is that y–you?!" she stammered.

The two white horses turned around and nodded, their eyes dazzled with shock. But

by the look of the horns coming out of her cousins' heads, they weren't horses at all – they were unicorns!

Isabelle, who had a curly, bright red mane and tail, just like her hair, began trotting around. "This is AMAZING!" she cried. "We're unicorns!"

But Cora was shaking her head frantically, making her golden mane swoosh from side to side. "No, no, no – I must be imagining this! It must be the jet lag. It can't be real!"

Lei noticed a shallow pool of water behind them, in the shadows of the mountainside, and had an idea. She nudged Cora towards it. "Look at your reflection. It IS real!"

Cora slowly trotted over to the pool, and Isabelle joined her. The shadows seemed to brighten as the three of them bent their

heads to look at the water.

"Magic," Isabelle whispered as three long unicorn heads stared back at them from the pool.

Lei kicked out her front hooves in excitement as she noticed her mane. "I have pink hair!" she cried.

Isabelle pointed her head at Lei's bottom and neighed. "And a pink tail!" Isabelle began trotting along the mountain path, feeling the spring in her step each time her hooves hit the ground. She'd always loved riding ponies – but actually *being* a unicorn was even better. Her white coat seemed to fizz with energy, and she felt warm and happy.

Lei left the pool to follow Isabelle. "Where are we?" she asked again as they cantered along together. It felt strange to be travelling on four legs, but really natural, too – like her legs knew exactly what to do as they moved steadily along the path. "Who do you think lives here?"

Cora galloped towards her cousins and

snorted anxiously. "And how will we get back to our families? They'll soon notice we're missing, and we said we'd be back for the barbie!"

Isabelle turned around and trotted back to Cora. "Um, I'm not sure," Isabelle said. "But try not to panic."

Cora had stopped now, her blue eyes clouded with worry, and Isabelle nuzzled her head into her neck to comfort her. As she pulled away, Isabelle spotted something in the rock. "What's that?" she asked, pawing at the ground with her hoof.

Lei galloped over, and saw what Isabelle meant. In the rock, there were more smooth hoof shapes. "Maybe this is how we get home!"

Cora tilted her head, looking unsure. "What do you mean?"

 Would you like more animal puzzles and activities?

 Want sneak peeks of other books in the series, including the Owls and Unicorns of Blossom Wood?

 Fancy flying across the treetops in the magical Blossom Wood game?

Then check out the Blossom Wood and Blossom Meadow website at:

blossomwoodbooks.com